MW01324740

EYE TO EYE WITH DOGS

MINIATURE SCHNAUZERS

Lynn M. Stone

Publishing LLC
Vero Beach, Florida 32964

www.rourkepublishing.com

PHOTO CREDITS: All photos © Lynn M. Stone

Editor: Robert Stengard-Olliges

Cover and page design by Nicola Stratford

Library of Congress Cataloging-in-Publication Data

Stone, Lynn M.
Miniature schnauzers / Lynn M. Stone.
p. cm. -- (Eye to eye with dogs)
Includes index.
ISBN 1-60044-236-6
1. Miniature schnauzer--Juvenile literature. I. Title. II. Series: Stone, Lynn M. Eye to eye with dogs.
SF429.M58S76 2007
636.755--dc22

2006010673

Printed in the USA

CG/CG

Rourke Publishing

www.rourkepublishing.com – sales@rourkepublishing.com
Post Office Box 3328, Vero Beach, FL 32964

1-800-394-7055

Table of Contents

Miniature schnauzer wears a long, flowing beard.

The Miniature Schnauzer

Don't let its old-man-of-the-mountain beard fool you! The miniature schnauzer is always a youngster at heart. Playful and active without being out of control, miniature schnauzers are also affectionate and bright.

MINIATURE SCHNAUZER FACTS

Weight: 13 – 15 pounds (6 – 7 kg)
Height: 12 – 14 inches (31 – 36 cm)
Country of Origin: Germany
Life Span: 12 – 14 years

The miniature schnauzer is a smaller version of the standard and giant schnauzers. First **bred** in Germany, Schnauzers are named for their long snout, the German word for which is *schnauze*.

Schnauzer breeds were named for their long snouts.

The modern miniature schnauzer, knee-high to its master, is a fine companion dog.

The miniature schnauzer is one of the terrier **breeds**. Like other terriers, they were originally used as "ratters" – dogs used to catch rats. Miniature schnauzers are no longer ratters. Today they are one of the most popular of companion dogs.

On the alert, a miniature schnauzer trots along a fenced backyard.

Schnauzers do well in country settings as well as in cities.

Leaping the hurdle on an agility course is good exercise for a miniature schnauzer.

The Dog for You?

Most miniature schnauzers are not as noisy, snappy, nor as excitable as other terrier breeds. People who want a small, calm dog may like the miniature schnauzer. Its alertness makes it a fine watchdog, and schnauzers tend to love children.

The miniature schnauzer's small size makes it ideal for city living, but it can also be a "country" dog. After all, miniature schnauzers are rugged little dogs. They withstand both warm and moderately cold weather well. They love physical activity and do well on **agility courses**. They should be regularly exercised on-leash or in fenced backyards. However, they should be kept indoors. They require plenty of human attention.

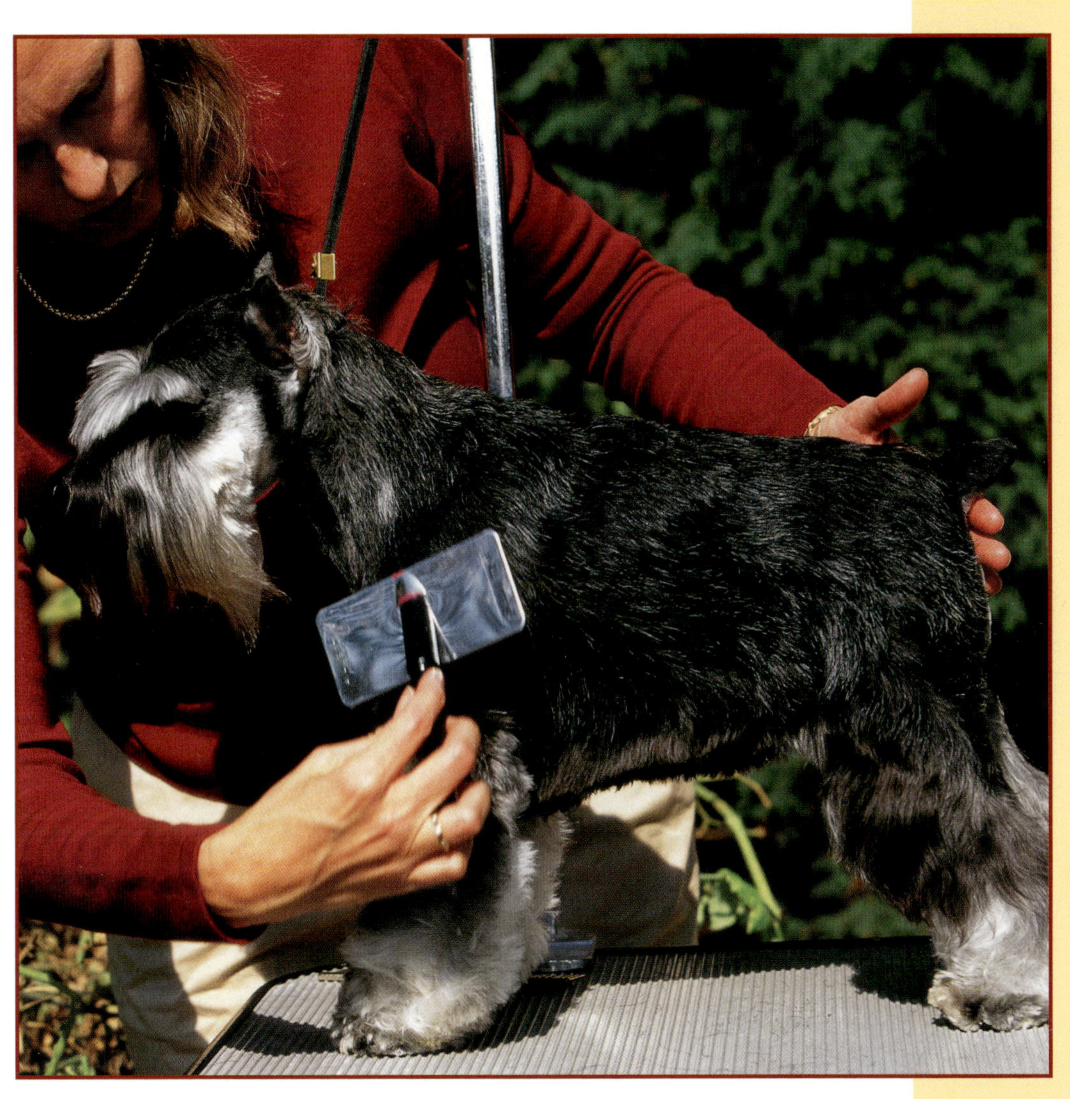

A miniature schnauzer stands patiently for grooming.

The schnauzer's wiry coat needs combing at least once weekly. The coats of **conformation** show dogs require regular grooming attention for cutting and shaping.

Schnauzers are the only terriers without roots in the British Isles.

Good-natured schnauzers have become a popular U.S. breed.

Miniature Schnauzers of the Past

German breeders developed the miniature schnauzer in the late 1800's to catch rats. The miniature schnauzer probably resulted from crossing standard schnauzers and miniature pinschers. The "full size" schnauzers go back to at least the 1400's.

Unlike other dogs in the terrier group, the schnauzer is the only one whose roots are not in the British Isles. Also unlike some of the British terriers, the schnauzer tends to be a naturally happy dog.

Early owners of miniature schnauzers liked the breed for qualities other than ratting. By 1925, the breed had become settled in the United States.

With chew toy in mouth, a miniature schnauzer invites its owner to play.

This well-groomed schnauzer is ready for the show.

Today the miniature schnauzer is much more popular than the larger schnauzer breeds. It is one of the most popular of all dogs in North America.

Looks

A well-groomed miniature schnauzer is a distinctive dog that stands from 12 to 14 inches (31 – 36 centimeters). It has a trim, sturdy body, but it is the dog's appearance that draws attention, especially the bushy beard and bristly eyebrows. The schnauzer has a double coat. The outer hair is wiry and the undercoat is tight and soft.

Miniature schnauzers may be salt-and-pepper colored, black and silver, or solid black.

In the United States, miniature schnauzers usually have short, **docked** tails and **cropped**, upright ears.

Schnauzers have sharp ears and dark, almond-shaped eyes.

A Note about Dogs

Puppies are cute and cuddly, but only after serious thought should anybody buy one. Puppies, after all, grow up. Remember: A dog will require more than love and patience. It will need healthy food, exercise, grooming, medical care, and a safe place to live.

A dog can be your best friend, but you need to be its best friend, too.

Choosing the right breed for you requires homework. For more information about buying and owning a dog, contact the American Kennel Club or the Canadian Kennel Club.

Glossary

agility course (uh JIL uh tee KORSS) – a series of activities requiring athletic ability

bred (BRED) – to have been raised; to have been developed for a certain purpose or look

breed (BREED) – a particular kind of domestic animal within a larger, closely related group, such as the miniature schnauzer breed within the dog group

conformation (kon for MAY shuhn) – the desired look and structure of a dog (or other animal)

cropped (KROPT) – to have been cut and set to get a certain look, such as the ears of some dogs

docked (DOKT) – to have had a section or all of a tail removed

Index

Further Reading

American Kennel Club. *The Complete Dog Book*. American Kennel Club, 2006.
Furtsinger, Nancy. *Miniature Schnauzers*. ABDO Publishing, 2006.
Rayner, Matthew. *Dog.* Gareth Stevens Publishing, 2004.

Website to Visit

American Kenel Club – http://www.akc.org
Canadian Kenel Club – http://www.ckc.ca
The Miniature Schnauzer Club – http://amsc.us

About the Author

Lynn M. Stone is the author of more than 400 children's books. He is a talented natural history photographer as well. Lynn, a former teacher, travels worldwide to photograph wildlife in its natural habitat.